The Impossible Bridge

The Engineers' Report

by Jane Buxton
photographs by Jamie Lean

Learning Media®

Monday, March 10: 2:17 P.M.

In math last week, we began to build
a scale model of our town.
We started by using bits and pieces
we brought from home.
But we soon ran out of room,
so Clementine got a strip of cardboard
to make a bridge to the next table.
It looked all right,
but when Emma put a car on it,
the bridge bent in the middle.

Matt tried two strips of card,
but the bridge still wasn't strong enough.
He said that it was impossible to build a bridge
out of cardboard.
Emma said she would look on the Internet
for some information about bridges.

Tuesday, March 11: 10:04 A.M.

Emma told us what she had found on the Internet.
The bridge Clementine tried to make yesterday is called a **beam** bridge.
We decided to see if an **arch** bridge would be strong enough to join the two tables.
We used the same two strips of cardboard, and it worked really well.

Wednesday, March 12: 11:37 A.M.

Our teacher, Mr. Keith, gave us some different materials to work with – some plastic drinking straws, some Popsicle sticks, some sticky tape, and more cardboard. We made arch bridges and beam bridges and tried them with different cars and trucks. Mr. Keith asked us if we would like to write an engineers' report about our work.

Engineers' Report
Wednesday, March 12

Problem

To build a bridge strong enough
to hold toy cars and trucks.

What we did

We built a beam bridge
out of thin cardboard.
It wasn't strong enough.
We built an arch bridge
out of the same cardboard,
and it was strong enough.

What we found out

The arch bridge was much
stronger than the beam bridge.

Thursday, March 13: 10:57 A.M.

Today we decided to make a bigger bridge – from the table to the art trolley. Clementine used the straws to make a small bridge with a triangle on each side, but it was far too short to reach across the gap. So I made some triangles out of Popsicle sticks, and Emma, Luke, and Matt made triangles too.

When we joined all of our pieces together, the bridge was just the right length, and it was strong too.

Great Ideas for Totem poles

Engineers' Report
Thursday, March 13

Problem
To build bridges for our cars
to get from the table
to the art trolley.

What we did
We made bridges out of triangles.

What we found out
You can make a strong bridge
using triangle shapes.
You can join triangles together
to make a "truss."
A truss can make a bridge
really strong.

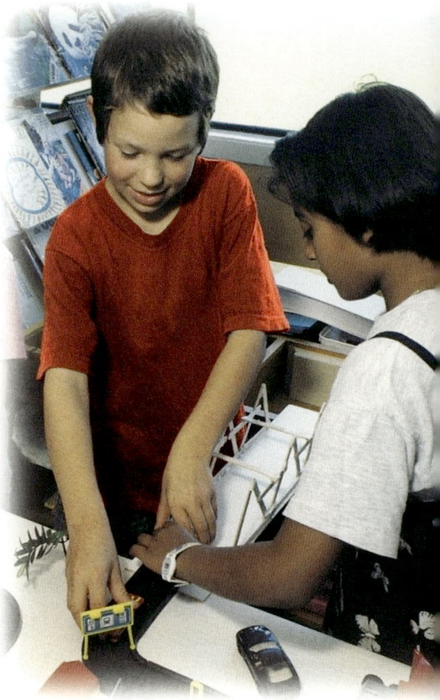

Friday, March 14: 1:57 P.M.

Today, after music,
we made a **suspension** bridge
from our table to Mr. Keith's table.

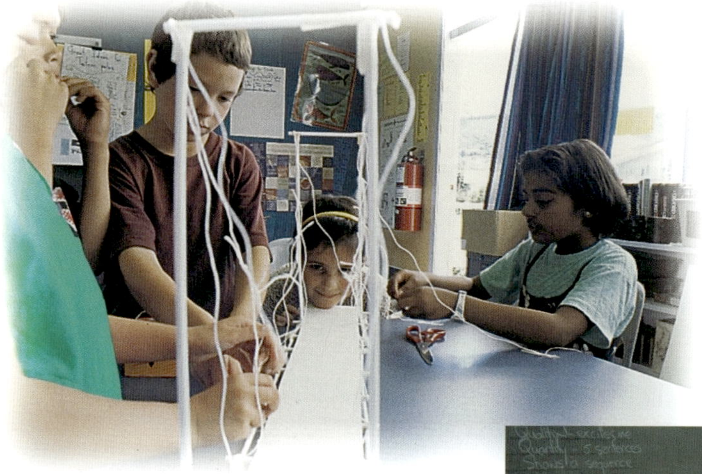

The bridge took
ages to make,
but it looked awesome.
This is what we said in our report.

Engineers' Report
Friday, March 14

Problem
To build a bridge long enough
to get from our table
to Mr. Keith's table.

What we did
We used drinking straws,
cardboard, and string.
We used sticky tape
to fix the strings
to both tables.

What we found out
The strings hold the bridge up.
A suspension bridge is really good
for going over a long gap.

Monday, March 17: 9:05 A.M.

Mr. Keith has given us a challenge.
This morning at math,
he gave us each one sheet
of A4 paper to make a bridge with.
We can cut or tear the paper only once,
and we can't use sticky tape.
It has to be strong enough to support
a toy car without bending.

Clementine, Matt, and Luke
say it can't be done – it's impossible.
Paper just isn't strong enough.
But Emma and I know some ways
of folding paper to make it stronger.
The others are all watching
to see what we do …

What would you do?

Engineers' Report

Monday, March 17

Problem

To build the impossible bridge

What we did ...